Splish-Splash Spring!

By Liza Alexander

Illustrated by Joe Ewers

A Random House PICTUREBACK® Book

Random House 🏠 New York

"Sesame Workshop,"® "Sesame Street,"® and associated characters, trademarks, and design elements are owned and licensed by Sesame Workshop. © 1989, 2000, 2016 by Sesame Workshop. All rights reserved. Published in the United States by Random House Children's Books, a division of Penguin Random House LLC, 1745 Broadway, New York, NY 10019, and in Canada by Random House of Canada, a division of Penguin Random House Ltd., Toronto, in conjunction with Sesame Workshop. Originally published in slightly different form by Golden Books in 1989 and by Random House Children's Books in 2000. Pictureback, Random House, and the Random House colophon are registered trademarks of Penguin Random House LLC.
Visit us on the Web!
randomhousekids.com
SesameStreetBooks.com
www.sesamestreet.org
Educators and librarians, for a variety of teaching tools, visit us at RHTeachersLibrarians.com
ISBN 978-1-101-93429-6 (trade) — ISBN 978-1-101-93430-2 (ebook)
Printed in the United States of America
10 9 8 7 6 5 4 3 2
Random House Children's Books supports the First Amendment and celebrates the right to read.

Splish-splashy day!
Let's go out and play!

Fat clouds in the sky
Shower rain on passersby.

Raindrops sprinkle hands and faces.
Puddles swell in empty places.

Float and swim, Rubber Duck!

Splish-splash by, muddy truck!

See the lightning? Hear the thunder!
Umbrellas up and all get under!

Shiny cars swoosh down the street.
Galoshes slosh upon our feet.

Foggy mist makes monsters dizzy.
Grover's fur gets wet and frizzy.

Get dry inside, out of the rain.
It pit-pats on the windowpane.

Tulips lift bright heads and listen.
Green leaves drink and drip and glisten.

Dark trees dip and bend and sway.
They dance away the rainy day.

Rainy days are full of fun.

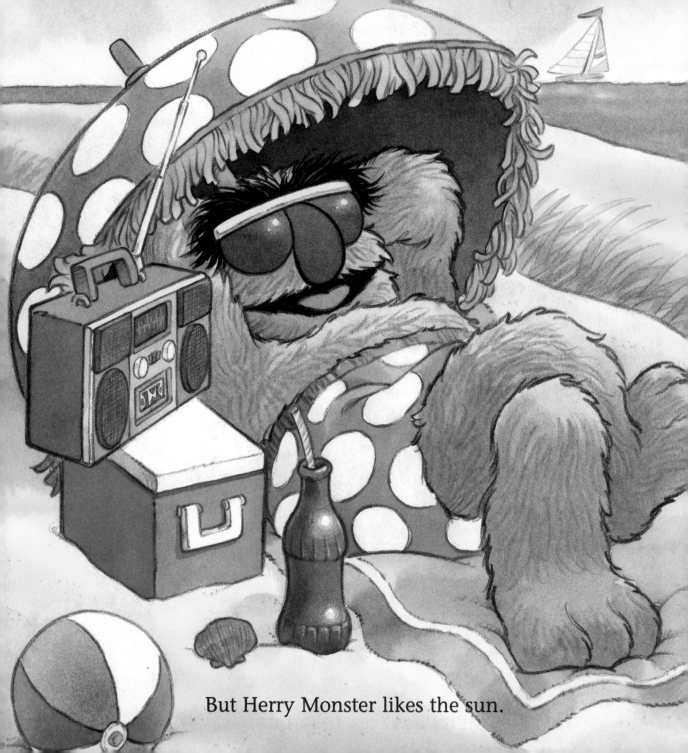

But Herry Monster likes the sun.